LAST CARTRIDGE: An
End To An Era

Copyright

Dedication

To my beloved family, who have always been my constant source of support and inspiration, I dedicate this book.

Your unwavering love and encouragement have fueled my passion for writing, and I am eternally grateful for your belief in me.

To my friends, whose laughter and camaraderie have lifted my spirits on the darkest of days, thank you for your unwavering friendship.

You have accompanied me on this journey of creativity and growth, and I am blessed to have you in my life.

To my mentors and colleagues, whose guidance and wisdom have shaped me into the writer I am today, I am indebted to your expertise and generosity.

Your invaluable feedback and constructive criticism have propelled me forward in my pursuit of excellence.

To all those who have touched my life in one way or another, thank you for being a part of my story.

This book is dedicated to each and every one of you, for without your influence, it would not have been possible.

May these words serve as a token of my gratitude and appreciation for your unwavering support.

Chapter 1: The Unseen Empire

As the sultry air of the bustling Mexican border town hung heavy with tension, Aaron Jones stood stoically, taking in the chaotic dance of street vendors and hustlers below. His keen eyes, hidden behind aviator sunglasses, scanned the scene, taking note of the covert transactions and clandestine dealings taking place in the shadows.

Aaron was no stranger to the seedy underbelly of this town. Having been an ex-Marine, he was no stranger to conflict and danger. Now, as a DEA operative, he was determined to bring justice to this lawless land. His rugged features were lined with determination, a reflection of the relentless pursuit of justice that burned within him.

He had honed his skills over the years, mastering the art of deciphering coded messages in criminal databases and exposing the intricate web of illicit activities that fueled the cartel's power. But beneath his steely facade, Aaron harbored a festering obsession with taking down the cartel once and for all.

His mind drifted back to the early days of his career, memories of his first encounters with the ruthless drug lords and the devastating impact of their operations on the community. He had made it his mission to dismantle their operations, taking down their men one by one. But the cartel was like a hydra, always growing new heads to replace the ones that were lost.

As the sun began to dip below the horizon, Aaron received a hint from an anonymous on Gloria Rum. The name sent a chill down his spine, sparking a fire in his belly. Something about this woman felt different, dangerous.

Without hesitation, Aaron set out to gather more information on Gloria Rum, determined to unravel the mystery surrounding this enigmatic figure. The stakes were higher than ever, and Aaron sensed that this could be the breakthrough he had been waiting for in his relentless pursuit of justice.

The sultry air of the border town may have been thick with tension, but Aaron was undeterred. With a steely gaze and a heart ablaze with determination, he marched forward, ready to take on whatever challenges lay ahead in his quest to bring down the cartel and bring peace to the troubled land.

Aaron Jones reached for the his fingers hovered with resolve over the sleek surface of his smartphone. The myriad of numbers and names scrolled past in a blur until he found the one that marked the start of his quest—a number shrouded in shadow and rumor, belonging to the famed investigative journalist known for unraveling enigmatic trails, Becky Fit.

He pressed the call button, the mundane beep of the dial tone undercut with the weight of his determination. Every ring chimed like the start of a countdown, the sound echoing his racing heartbeat. When Becky answered, her voice was a mixture of curiosity and nonchalance. "Aaron," she started, recognition tinted with surprise, "What sparked this call?"

Without preamble, Aaron explained, "Gloria Rum. It's time to find her. All paths we've ignored, every stone unturned—it ends now. She has slipped through the legal system's fingers far too long."

Becky silence on the other end was not of hesitation but of a cooling steeling. "I assume you're aware of what it means to chase someone like Rum? This goes beyond skipping town. She's a master at playing lost and found."

Aaron's reply was a granite firm, Becky gave a quiet assent, "Okay then. We'll need to be methodical. I'll reactivate old contacts and gather new intel. Rum is cunning, she leaves a wake of false leads. Prepare for a marathon, not a sprint."

phone. It was time to pull the thread. The hunt for Gloria Rum had begun.

Chapter 2: The Insider

Richardson Smith had risen through the ranks of the notorious cartel with ruthless determination. His reputation as a high-ranking member was matched only by the fear he inspired in his enemies.

But deep down, Richardson was disillusioned by the violence and betrayal that defined his world. The constant bloodshed and ruthless competition had taken its toll, leaving him with a gnawing sense of disillusionment and guilt.

Desperate for a way out, Richardson decided to reach out to Aaron, an experienced federal agent, with compromising information that could bring down the entire cartel. In exchange for immunity and protection, Richardson was willing to risk his life and betray the very organization that had once been his lifeblood.

Their secret meeting was tense and filled with the palpable threat of danger. Richardson confessed that he was the anonymous that gave him an hint on Gloria Rum.

He then nervously handed over a trove of incriminating evidence and insider knowledge, knowing that doing so labeled him a traitor in the eyes of his former comrades. Aaron, for his part, knew that protecting Richardson would not be easy—the cartel had eyes and ears everywhere, and they would stop at nothing to silence their turncoat insider.

As the wheels of justice began to turn, Richardson found himself constantly looking over his shoulder, jumping at every unexpected noise. He knew that his decision had put a target on his back and that the cartel would not rest until they had exacted their revenge.

The authorities, on the other hand, worked feverishly to build a case against the cartel, using Richardson's information as a starting point.

With each passing day, the noose tightened around the organization, leading to a series of high-profile arrests and seizures. The downfall of the cartel seemed inevitable, but it came with a high price for Richardson.

As the cartel's grip on power began to slip, their desperation turned to fury, and Richardson found himself in the crosshairs of their wrath. Despite the protection offered by the authorities, he lived in constant fear, never knowing when or where the cartel's retribution would strike.

In the end, Richardson's decision to betray his former comrades led to the dismantling of the cartel, but the cost was immeasurable. He had traded one form of danger for another, and the guilt of what he had done weighed heavily on his conscience.

The downfall of the cartel was a victory for law and order, but it came with a heavy toll for Richardson. As he looked out at the world beyond the bars of his new life in witness protection, he couldn't help but wonder if the price of his freedom was too high. But in the end, he knew that there was no going back, and he could only hope that his sacrifice had made the world a better place.

Chapter 3: The Journalist's Lead

Becky Rit, a seasoned investigative journalist, always had a nose for sniffing out the truth. So when she stumbled upon a series of suspicious financial transactions in her research, she knew she had struck gold.

Her digging led her to the seemingly legitimate businesswoman, Gloria Rum. However, Becky soon discovered that Gloria was nothing but a front for the cartel's money laundering operations. The complexities of the shell companies and the way the money was being funneled through Gloria's business left Becky in awe of the cartel's cunning tactics.

But Becky was not one to be intimidated. Her relentless pursuit of the truth led to Aaron, a highly regarded law enforcement official, taking notice of her work. As Becky dug deeper into Gloria's involvement with the cartel, she realized that she had caught the attention of some dangerous individuals.

Despite the risks, Becky continued to follow the trail of laundered money, determined to expose the truth and bring Gloria and her nefarious cohorts to justice. Her unwavering commitment to her investigation and her steadfast determination to reveal the truth drew admiration from Aaron, who saw her as a force to be reckoned with.

As Becky's investigation into the cartel gained momentum, she quickly found herself wading into dangerous waters. The more she poked around, the more the cartel became aware of her meddling, and they began to take drastic measures to silence her. But Becky was not the type to back down easily. She knew that the truth was too important to be silenced.

As the web of deceit and danger closed in around her, Becky's courage and determination never wavered. She continued to dig deeper, uncovering the intricate details of the cartel's elaborate money laundering scheme. But as she got closer to the truth, the threats against her only grew stronger.

Despite the danger, Becky refused to be intimidated. She knew that the information she had could save countless lives, and she was not about to let fear get in the way of that. With each new discovery, she meticulously pieced together the evidence, and before long, she had enough to blow the case wide open.

Her exposé not only brought the cartel's illegal activities to light, but it also dismantled their entire operation. Countless lives were saved because of Becky's unwavering pursuit of the truth. She had become a legend in the world of investigative journalism, and her story inspired others to take a stand against corruption and injustice.

Becky's determination and fearlessness had not only made her a hero, but they had also made her a force to be reckoned with. The cartel may have tried to silence her, but in the end, they were no match for her unwavering determination and commitment to uncovering the truth.

Chapter 4: The Innocent Facade

Gloria Rum was not your average woman. With her sharp wit and magnetic charm, she could easily sweep anyone off their feet. But beneath her charismatic facade lay a cunning mind, always aware that she was under scrutiny.

Becky, a seasoned investigator, had been on the trail of Gloria for months. She had a hunch that Gloria was involved in some shady dealings, but every time she tried to dig deeper, Gloria would seamlessly evade her questions with a well-timed joke or a sly smile. It was maddening, but Becky couldn't help but admire Gloria's quick thinking and silver tongue.

Meanwhile, Aaron, another investigator, had also been on Gloria's tail. He was determined to uncover her secrets and bring her to justice. But every time he thought he had a lead, Gloria would slip through his fingers with a smooth excuse or a flirtatious wink.

Gloria knew she was walking a fine line, and she relished the challenge of outsmarting both Becky and Aaron. She was well aware of their relentless pursuit, but she remained unfazed. After all, she had spent years honing her skills at evading detection, and she was not about to let a couple of nosy investigators bring her down.

It wasn't long before Becky's investigation led her to a chance encounter with Alexandria Gota, a high-ranking member of a notorious cartel. As they conversed, Becky couldn't help but notice a hint of vulnerability in Alexandria's eyes when she mentioned Gloria's name. It was a crack in Gloria's armor, and Becky knew she had to exploit it.

Meanwhile, Aaron's investigation took an unexpected turn when he stumbled upon a secret meeting where Gloria was suspected to be present. But once again, she managed to slip away before he could get a clear view of her. Frustrated but undeterred, Aaron redoubled his efforts to track her down.

But Gloria was always one step ahead. She used her charm and quick thinking to navigate through the dangerous world she inhabited, and she made sure that neither Becky nor Aaron could pin her down. As the investigations intensified, Gloria played a dangerous game of cat and mouse, reveling in the thrill of outmaneuvering her would-be captors.

In the end, Gloria Rum remained elusive, her true nature shrouded in mystery. While Becky and Aaron continued to pursue her, Gloria simply laughed, knowing that she had once again evaded their grasp with her charm and wit. And as she vanished into the shadows, she promised herself that she would always stay one step ahead- no matter who tried to catch her.

Chapter 5: Crossing Paths

In a world where alliances are fleeting and trust is a rare commodity, an uneasy partnership takes shape. Marked by mutual trust and bound by a shared objective, Aaron and Becky find themselves drawn into a collaboration born out of necessity.

Recognizing the need for strategic insight, they decide to leverage Richardson's knowledge, the cartel's chief strategist and Alexandria's right-hand man.

Richardson's intricate understanding of the Last Cartel's inner workings becomes a pivotal asset in their pursuit. The decision is made to set a trap for Gloria Rum, a former cartel member with a vendetta and a hidden arsenal of dangerous secrets.

The dynamics of this alliance are defined by a delicate balance. Aaron, a seasoned DEA operative, brings tactical skills and a background in navigating the complexities of criminal enterprises. On the other hand, Becky, a tenacious investigate journalist contributes her analytical prowess in unraveling the financial intricacies that underpin the cartel's operations.

The uneasy alliance takes shape in the shadows, where every exchanged glance and shared secret is tinged with suspicion. As they delve deeper into the world of cartel intrigue, Aaron and

Becky must navigate not only the external threats but also the internal uncertainties that come with working alongside someone with their own agenda.

In the high-stakes world of espionage, trust is a rare commodity. Richardson and his team knew this all too well as they sat around the table, plotting their next move against the infamous Gloria Rum. Richardson possessed valuable knowledge that could bring Rum to her knees, but the risk of betrayal was always lurking in the shadows.

As they meticulously orchestrated the elements of their trap, every step was fraught with the potential for betrayal. The tension in the room rose with each passing moment, mirroring the precarious nature of their collaboration. They knew that one wrong move could lead to their downfall, but they pressed on, fueled by the thrill of the chase and the desire for justice.

Their plan was cunning and meticulously thought out, relying on Richardson's knowledge of Rum's inner circle and their vulnerabilities. They knew that if they played their cards right, they could finally bring an end to Rum's reign of terror.

But as they put their plan into action, the stakes only grew higher. Each decision they made felt like a gamble, and the consequences of failure weighed heavy on their shoulders. They navigated through a web of double-crosses and false leads, their trust in each other the only thing keeping them afloat in a sea of deception.

As the day of reckoning drew near, the tension reached a fever pitch. Every move they made was a calculated risk, and the fate of their mission hung in the balance. The trap was set, and all they could do was wait and hope that their gamble would pay off.

Their plan to use Richardson's knowledge to set a trap for Gloria Rum was a high-stakes gambit that tested the limits of their trust and resolve.

Chapter 6: The Mole

As Alexandria Gota makes her rounds through the dark and dingy alleyways of the city, she couldn't shake the feeling that something was off about Richardson, one of the most trusted members of the cartel. His behavior had become increasingly erratic, and his frequent disappearances had raised red flags in Alexandria's mind.

As the appointed enforcer of the cartel's rules, Alexandria was responsible for maintaining order and ensuring that no one stepped out of line. It was her duty to root out any potential traitors within their ranks, and Richardson's suspicious behavior had put her on high alert.

Determined to uncover the truth, Alexandria started her own shadow operation, using her knowledge of the city's underworld to gather information and keep a close eye on Richardson's movements. She knew that if there was a traitor in their midst, it could mean the downfall of the entire cartel, and she wasn't about to let that happen on her watch.

As she delved deeper into her investigation, Alexandria's loyalty and cunning were put to the test. She knew she had to tread carefully, as any misstep could lead to dire consequences. But with each passing day, her suspicion of Richardson grew stronger, and she was determined to uncover his secret at any cost.

It wasn't long before Alexandria's efforts paid off, and she finally discovered the truth about Richardson's betrayal. As she confronted him, the tension in the air was thick, and she could see the fear in his eyes as he realized that his betrayal had been uncovered.

With a heavy heart, Alexandria knew that she had no choice but to uphold the cartel's rules. Richardson, a longtime friend and compatriot, had betrayed the organization and put them all at risk. Despite her feelings of loyalty and friendship, Alexandria made the difficult decision to hand Richardson over to the cartel leader El Diablo for punishment.

As she watched the leaders take Richardson away, Alexandria felt a pang of guilt and sadness. She had grown up with Richardson in the streets, and they had been through so much together. But in the world of organized crime, loyalty was everything, and betrayal could not go unpunished.

Still, Alexandria couldn't shake the feeling of unease that lingered in her heart. She knew she had done the right thing, but it weighed heavily on her conscience. Her unwavering determination and sharp instincts had saved the cartel from the threat of a traitor within their midst, but it came at a heavy price.

Returning to her duties as the cartel's enforcer, Alexandria pushed aside her doubts and focused on proving her loyalty and cunning once again. She knew that she had solidified her place as a force to be reckoned with in the dangerous world of organized crime, but the guilt of betraying Richardson lingered in the back of her mind.

As the days passed, Alexandria couldn't shake the feeling of emptiness that had settled in her heart. She had done what she had to do, but it didn't make it any easier. With a heavy heart, she continued to carry out her duties, knowing that in the world of organized crime, there was no room for sentimentality.

Chapter 7: The Network Unraveled

Becky had been working as an undercover agent for the federal government for years, but she had never received a tip quite like this one. It was a private message on her secure line, and the sender was anonymous. The message contained detailed information about a high-level meeting within the cartel, set to take place in just a few days. The tipster claimed to be a former member of the cartel who had turned informant, and they were willing to provide Becky with the information she needed to bring down some of the biggest players in the organization.

Becky knew she couldn't ignore this tip, but she also knew she couldn't pursue it alone. She needed a partner she could trust implicitly, someone who was as skilled in undercover work as she was. That's when she called Aaron, her longtime partner in the field. They had been through countless dangerous operations together, and she knew he was the only one she could count on for a mission like this.

After carefully analyzing the information provided by the anonymous tipster, Becky and Aaron devised a plan to infiltrate the meeting. They would pose as buyers interested in making a deal with the cartel, using the information they had been given to gain access to the inner circle of the organization. They spent days perfecting their cover stories, memorizing every detail of the operation, knowing that the slightest mistake could cost them their lives.

As the day of the meeting arrived, Becky and Aaron made their way to the secluded location, feeling the weight of the mission ahead of them. They were met with suspicious eyes and veiled threats, but they remained calm and composed, playing their roles to perfection. As the meeting progressed, they observed the key figures in the cartel discussing their illegal operations and making plans for future criminal activities.

It was a tense and nerve-wracking situation, they managed to obtain vital evidence that would expose the cartel's top members. Just as they were about to leave, a sudden commotion erupted as the cartel leaders became aware of their true identities. Becky and Aaron had been compromised, and they found themselves in a life-threatening situation.

In a heart-pounding escape, They narrowly evaded danger, using their training to navigate through the labyrinthine corridors of the cartel's compound. They managed to make it to safety with the evidence in hand, knowing that they had succeeded in their mission. The information they had obtained would be enough to bring down the cartel's key figures and dismantle the entire organization.

They returned to their superiors, presenting the evidence they had risked their lives to obtain. The cartel's leaders were swiftly apprehended, and the organization crumbled without its key figures at the helm. The anonymous tip had led to a critical breakthrough in the war against organized crime, and Becky and Aaron had played a pivotal role in bringing justice to those who had terrorized communities for far too long.

As they looked back on the operation, they knew they had made a difference, but they also knew that their work was far from over. The fight against criminal organizations would always require brave and dedicated individuals like themselves, but they were ready to take on whatever challenges lay ahead, knowing that they were making the world a safer place for everyone.

Chapter 8: Breaking Point

Gloria had always prided herself on her ability to stay cool under pressure. As the head of a powerful criminal network, she had made countless difficult decisions and navigated treacherous situations with ease. But when a series of unexpected setbacks rocked her empire, she found herself making rash choices that attracted the attention of law enforcement.

With the net closing in around her, Gloria turned to her close confidant, Ashley Bing, for support. Ashley was a tech genius who had played a crucial role in maintaining the digital infrastructure of the criminal network. As law enforcement zeroed in on Gloria, it became clear that Ashley's involvement in the network's activities could no longer be concealed.

As the pressure mounted, Gloria's rash decisions led to a series of high-profile encounters with law enforcement. Each close call only served to increase her desperation and drive her to make even riskier moves. But as Gloria's world began to unravel, Ashley found herself facing a dilemma of her own.

For years, Ashley had faithfully served as Gloria's right-hand woman, using her technological prowess to keep the criminal network running smoothly. But as the authorities closed in, Ashley began to question her loyalty to Gloria. She knew that if she continued to support Gloria, she risked being implicated in the network's illegal activities. On the other hand, turning on Gloria could have even more dire consequences.

In a moment of clarity, Ashley made the decision to become a wildcard in the unfolding drama. She reached out to law enforcement and offered to provide them with crucial information about the criminal network's digital infrastructure. In exchange for immunity, Ashley began to unravel the complex web of technology that had allowed the network to operate with impunity for so long.

As Gloria's world came crashing down around her, Ashley's actions proved to be the final blow. With the evidence provided by Ashley, law enforcement was able to dismantle the criminal network and bring Gloria to justice. As Gloria faced the consequences of her actions, Ashley was left to ponder her own role in the downfall of the woman she had once considered a friend.

In the end, both women had been forced to make difficult decisions under pressure. While Gloria had let desperation lead her down a path of reckless choices, Ashley had ultimately chosen to step out of the shadows and take a stand against the criminal activities that had once defined her life. Their choices had ultimately shaped their fates in unexpected ways, leaving them to grapple with the consequences of their actions for years to come.

Chapter 9: The Dominoes Fall

As the sun began to set over the rugged terrain of the Mexican countryside, the sound of helicopters could be heard in the distance. The coordinated strike by the DEA was about to unfold, based on the evidence gathered over months of grueling undercover work and surveillance. In a matter of hours, the impending collapse of a major drug cartel would send shockwaves through the criminal underworld.

Gloria, a high-ranking member of the cartel, paced nervously in her luxurious villa, her mind racing with thoughts of the impending raid by the DEA. She had always been confident in her ability to outsmart the authorities, but now she felt a sense of impending doom like never before. As the sound of approaching helicopters grew louder, she made a desperate attempt to escape, only to be met with a team of heavily armed DEA agents at every turn. Her once formidable empire now lay in ruins as she was swiftly arrested and whisked away to face the consequences of her illicit deeds.

Meanwhile, Alexandria, a notorious enforcer for the cartel, reacted to the impending collapse in a completely different manner. Unwilling to face the possibility of capture and imprisonment, she made a daring escape through the winding backstreets of the city, narrowly evading the DEA agents hot on her trail. But even as she managed to outwit her pursuers,by trying to blend into the crowd, and using all her resources to evade capture. However, she was ultimately tracked down and taken into custody.

As the dust settled on the DEA's sweeping arrests, the fate of Richardson, a key informant within the cartel, hung precariously in the balance. Having been captured and tortured by the cartel for his treachery, he held on to the hope that the DEA would come through for him. And in a dramatic display of heroism, DEA operatives launched a daring rescue mission, risking their own lives to save Richardson from the clutches of the vengeful cartel.

The DEA's relentless pursuit of justice had finally paid off with the confession of Gloria Rum and Alexandria Gota, leading to the discovery of the leader of the cartel hiding in an underground tunnel in Santa Cruz, Mexico. With this information in hand, DEA operatives Aaron Jones and Becky Rit swung into action, coordinating a raid to take down the leader, El Diablo, and other top cartel members.

The successful rescue of Richardson, a DEA agent who had been held captive by the cartel, was a pivotal moment in the operation. With the arrests of El Diablo and his associates, the DEA dealt a devastating blow to the criminal organization, bringing a sense of hope and justice to the people of Mexico.

The long and arduous investigation had finally come to a triumphant conclusion, but the fallout of the coordinated strike would reverberate for years to come. The DEA's unwavering dedication and unyielding resolve had sent a clear message to the criminals: no one was beyond the reach of the law.

As the stars began to twinkle in the night sky, a new era was dawning in Mexico. The DEA's efforts had set the stage for a brighter future, where the rule of law reigned supreme and the people could live free from fear. The relentless pursuit of justice by the DEA agents became a beacon of optimism in a world that had long been shrouded in darkness.

The people of Mexico saw that justice was possible, and the DEA's relentless pursuit of the truth became a symbol of hope. As they continued their efforts to bring down the criminal underworld, the DEA agents knew that they were making a difference - one sunset at a time.

Chapter 10: Ashes to Ashes

The aftermath revealed the cartel's downfall and the high cost of the war on drugs. Aaron, couldn't help but feel a sense of emptiness.The streets were quieter, the prisons fuller, and the scars of the conflict evident on the faces of those who had fought on both sides. Aaron couldn't help but wonder if the victory was truly worth the sacrifices made.

Aaron grappled with these thoughts, Becky, an investigative journalist, was hard at work on her latest exposé. Her research had uncovered unexpected high-profile figures linked to the cartel, revealing a web of corruption that extended far beyond the borders of the country. Her findings hinted that the last cartel was just a piece of a larger puzzle, one that reached into the highest echelons of power.

Becky's exposé sparked outrage and disbelief among the public, but it also raised questions about the true extent of the war on drugs. As Aaron read her report, he couldn't shake the feeling that the victory over the last cartel was just a small battle in a much larger war. The revelations made him question whether the sacrifices made by him and his colleagues had truly made a difference, or if they were merely pawns in a game they could never hope to win.

Aaron and Becky's paths cross as they both come to realize that the war on drugs is far from over. Together, they vow to continue the fight, determined to uncover the truth and hold those responsible for the devastation accountable.

As they delve deeper into the murky world of drug trafficking and corruption, they find themselves up against powerful adversaries who will stop at nothing to protect their interests. But Aaron and Becky refuse to back down, knowing that the cost of inaction is far greater than the risks they face.

The story ends with a note of hope, as Aaron and Becky, along with their allies, stand united in their determination to bring about real change. They may have won the battle against the last cartel, but the war rages on, and they are ready to face whatever challenges lie ahead.

Printed in Great Britain
by Amazon

37957901R00030